What's the Matter with Albert?

A Story of Albert Einstein

Frieda Wishinsky

Illustrated by Jacques Lamontagne

MAPLE
TREE
PRESS

Dedication
For Bill, for always

Maple Tree Press Inc.
51 Front Street East, Suite 200, Toronto, Ontario M5E 1B3

Text © 2002 Frieda Wishinsky
Illustrations © 2002 Jacques Lamontagne

Distributed in the United States by Firefly Books (U.S.) Inc.
230 Fifth Avenue, Suite 1607, New York, NY 10001

We acknowledge the financial support of the Canada Council for the Arts, the Ontario Arts Council, and the Government of Canada through the Book Publishing Industry Development Program (BPIDP) for our publishing activities.

Cataloguing in Publication Data
Wishinsky, Frieda
    What's the matter with Albert? : a story of Albert Einstein

ISBN 1-894379-31-4 (bound)   ISBN 1-894379-32-2 (pbk.)

1. Einstein, Albert, 1879–1955—Juvenile literature. 2. Einstein, Albert, 1879–1955.
3. Physicists—Biography—Juvenile literature. 4. Physicists. I. Lamontage, Jacques, 1961–
II. Title.

QC16.E5W54 2002   530'.092   C2002-901020-9

Design & art direction: Word & Image Design Studio Inc. (www.wordandimagedesign.com)
Illustrations: Jacques Lamontagne

Photo Credits
Page 26: Hulton-Deutsch Collection/CORBIS/MAGMA; 27(top right), 30: Courtesy of the Archives, California Institute of Technology; 27(bottom left): The Albert Einstein Archives, The Hebrew University in Jerusalem, Israel.

Printed in Hong Kong

A   B   C   D   E   F

Who Was Albert Einstein?

Albert Einstein is one of the most famous scientists who ever lived. Why is he so famous? He didn't invent anything. He didn't discover a new planet or a star. He didn't produce something faster, bigger, or better.

What Albert Einstein did was see the world in a new way. He asked new questions about light, energy, space, time, mass, and gravity. He formulated new answers. He made scientists rethink their old theories and see new possibilities.

Some scientists have used Einstein's ideas to harness atomic energy. Engineers and inventors have used his ideas to create fluorescent light, television, and lasers. Astronomers have used his ideas to think about how the universe was formed, to estimate its size, and to wonder whether it is shrinking or growing.

Einstein didn't have answers to all his questions. For many years, he worked on finding a unified theory—a single explanation for how the universe works. In the end, he didn't find it. But Einstein was never discouraged. He believed that he was just one scientist adding one piece to a gigantic puzzle. He believed that we all have to look at the world as children do, with wonder and curiosity, and keep asking basic questions about how and why things happen.

Einstein was one of the most famous people in the world, but he didn't care about fame. He won many awards, but he didn't care about prizes or money. Einstein cared about ideas, and he also cared about making the world a more peaceful place. He spoke and wrote articles about democracy, freedom, and peace. He used his fame to warn the world about the dangers of dictatorships, nuclear weapons, and war.

Albert Einstein was a great scientist and humanitarian, but once he was just a boy.

Here is his story.

"Albert Einstein! You want *me* to interview Albert Einstein?"

"Billy," said our newspaper editor, Jane, "you want to be a reporter, don't you? How are you going to do that if you're scared to talk to people?"

"But ... but ..." I stammered. "This is different."

"An interview's an interview," said Jane, staring at me with her piercing eyes. Then her gaze softened a bit. "Don't worry. He won't bite."

How could I say no? After all, I was a new reporter for the *Princeton Elementary School News*. Interviewing people was my job. But this was different. It wasn't like interviewing Jim Black, our local policeman. Or even Dr. Ford, my doctor, who insisted on checking my tonsils while I was in her office. This was Albert Einstein, the smartest man in the world.

What could I say to him? How could I interview him? I was only a B– student in math, and that was *after* my mom had drilled me for hours on my multiplication tables.

"Go to see him today," said Jane. "We're printing the story on Friday."

"But what if he's busy?" I stammered. "What if he's not home? What if he doesn't want to talk to me?"

"You're a reporter, Billy." Jane stared down at me (she's a foot taller and two grades older). "Get your story!"

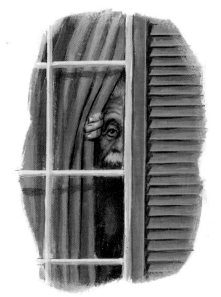

That's how I found myself knocking on Albert Einstein's door on a wet Tuesday afternoon after school. I knocked a couple of times, but no one answered. I waited on the covered porch for five minutes as the rain splashed down around me.

Just as I was about to give up, a curtain parted at one of the green-shuttered bottom windows. My breath caught in my throat. I heard footsteps coming toward me.

The door opened, and I knew who it was right away. The baggy pants, the moth-nibbled sweater, the scruffy shoes without socks, and the wiry hair all told me that Albert Einstein himself had answered the door.

"And who are you?" he asked in his thick German accent.

"I'm Billy Whitestone from the *Princeton Elementary School News* and could I please interview you for our paper?" I blurted out.

"A newspaper reporter?" said Dr. Einstein gruffly. "I don't usually give interviews."

"Oh," I said, not knowing what to do next. How could I tell Jane that I couldn't get the interview? I could almost hear her bark, "You're fired!"

Maybe it was the look on my face, or maybe it was just that Dr. Einstein was kind, but something made him change his mind. The next thing I knew, his gruff tone had disappeared and a soft twinkle sparkled in his eyes instead.

"Well," he said, "it *is* raining, and you've come all this way. Perhaps you'd like a cup of hot chocolate while we talk?"

"Would I!" I exclaimed, practically jumping.

"Then come in, Billy Whitestone, and ask me your questions."

I followed Dr. Einstein into his house. As he led me into the study, I looked around. There were books and papers piled everywhere. Dr. Einstein pointed me to one chair and then sat across from me in another.

"Tell me, then," he asked as his secretary, Helen Dukas, brought us two cups of hot chocolate with whipped cream. "What is it that you would like to know?"

I swallowed hard. "I would like to know what you were like when you were a boy," I answered. "Were you always the smartest student in your class?"

Albert Einstein laughed. "My teachers did not think I was so smart."

"Are you kidding?" I said.

"No. They often said, 'Stop daydreaming, Albert. Come back down to earth. Your head is stuck up in the clouds with the birds.'"

"And was it?" I asked.

"Yes, sometimes it was in the clouds. But not with the birds. Let me start from the beginning. Let tell you how it was when I was a boy."

I pulled out my notepad and pencil and got ready to write.

"I was born many years ago, on March 14, 1879. My parents were Hermann and Pauline Einstein, a Jewish couple. They lived in the small German town of Ulm. It was a place of old cathedrals and narrow streets, near the beautiful Danube River.

"Unfortunately, I was not as beautiful as the Danube. Or even as beautiful as most babies. When my mother first saw me, she shrieked, 'What's the matter with Albert? He has a big, pointy head. Is he normal?' Even my grandmother Helene was worried. 'He's much too fat!' she exclaimed. But despite my strange head and dumpling shape, I *was* normal. Gradually, I even began to look normal.

"My parents, though, didn't stay long enough in Ulm for me to run and play along its winding streets. My father's electric factory was not doing well, and he wanted to try his luck in a larger city. So within a year of my birth, we moved to the big, bustling city of Munich, Germany.

"Slowly, my father's business began to do better, but I was still a worry. By the age of two, I still hadn't started to talk. 'All the other children talk,' said my mother. 'What's the matter with Albert?' But nothing was the matter with me. I didn't talk because I wasn't ready to talk."

Dr. Einstein paused. "Am I going too fast, Billy? You haven't had any of your hot chocolate yet."

It was true, so I took a sip but asked him to continue his story.

"Well, once I started talking," said Dr. Einstein. "I had lots to say, especially about my new baby sister, Maja. 'What's that?' I asked my parents when I first saw the little bundle.

"'It's your new sister,' said my father.

"'Sister?' I didn't know what that was. 'Where are her wheels?' I asked. She looked like a toy, and my toys had wheels.

"'What's the matter with you, Albert?' my mother said, sighing. 'Why do you think the way you do?'

"Gradually, my parents got used to the strange questions I asked. 'That's just Albert,' they'd explain to their friends and relatives. 'Albert is Albert.'

"But what they didn't get used to were my tantrums. Once I was so angry at my violin teacher that I picked up a chair and threw it at her. She ran out shrieking in terror and never returned to our house.

"'What's the matter with you, Albert?' scolded my mother. 'You must learn to control your temper.'

"I tried—after all, I didn't like being scolded. And eventually, I didn't get so angry—at least most of the time. Most of the time, I was busy figuring out puzzles, building block towers, and making tall houses out of cards. Once I even built a fourteen-story house out of cards. Maja was very impressed.

"At the age of five," said Albert Einstein, "I found a new love." His face broke into a grin at the memory. "It all began with a small compass. My father brought it to me when I was sick in bed because he thought it would amuse me. I sat up and held the compass. I turned it to the right. I turned it to the left. I shook it like a rattle. I rolled it across my bed like a car. And I discovered that no matter what I did, the compass always pointed in the same direction.

"I was so amazed. 'Why does it do that?' I wondered. I knew there had to be an answer. And I also knew that one day I wanted to find that answer. With that small compass, my love of science began.

"It certainly did not begin at school. I was not a bad student, as some people have said, but I was a dreamy student.

"I also spoke slowly. Some people believed I was stupid because of my slow speech. But I spoke slowly because I thought about what I was going to say before I said it.

"And there were other things that made school hard for me. I didn't like the drills my teachers demanded. I didn't like to memorize because I did not have a good memory. When the teacher talked on and on, my mind would fly off like a balloon. I wondered about all sorts of things: How fast did light travel? What was time? How old was the universe?

"My teachers were not happy with all my dreaming. 'What's the matter with you, Albert?' they'd shout. 'Listen to the lesson. Pay attention!' But it was difficult to pay attention to drills and lectures. My mind was filled with too many questions.

"Then two special people came into my life.

"One was a poor medical student named Max Talmud, who came to our house every Thursday for dinner. Max was twenty-one and I was twelve, but we became friends. Max brought me books—exciting, popular books about science and math. My favorite was about geometry. From Max and that book, I learned that geometry is the math of circles, squares, and rectangles. In geometry, all the parts fit together like the pieces of a puzzle. The parts are in harmony, like beautiful music by Mozart. I immediately liked the geometry puzzle.

"And then there was my uncle Jakob. He introduced me to another kind of math—algebra. I remember his words: 'Algebra is a merry science,' Uncle Jakob said. 'We go hunting for a little animal whose name we don't know, so we call it X. When we bag our game, we pounce on it and give it its right name.'

"Uncle Jakob made algebra fun, and I loved hunting for the unknown X. Max and Uncle Jakob made math and science come alive for me. Once they opened the doors, I rushed in to learn more.

"Despite that, I still had more school and more problems. And then my father's business ran into trouble again. My family moved once more—this time to Milan, Italy. I didn't go with them. I was fifteen years old, and my parents insisted I stay behind and finish school in Germany. That was torture. I lived in a boarding house and was lonely for my family. I didn't like school, and school didn't like me either.

"I was so unhappy that I was often moody and angry. I didn't throw chairs as I had done when I was a child, but I was not pleasant in class. All I wanted to do was run to my family in Italy. It sounded beautiful from my father's letters. He described the warm sunshine, the good food, and the friendly people. It sounded so much nicer than sitting in class with strict, sour teachers."

The expression on Dr. Einstein's face changed, as if a dark cloud had passed over it. "I was so miserable at that school," he continued. "Finally, my doctor gave me a note saying I should leave school because my sadness was making me unhealthy. But I never had to use the note. Instead, the school asked me to leave because of my bad attitude.

"I was relieved that I'd soon be reunited with my family but ashamed to have failed and disappointed them. Still, when I peered out the train's window as it sped toward Italy, I wanted to shout for joy. I was free! Free from that awful school.

"The minute I arrived in Italy, I loved everything about it. I loved the hills and valleys inviting me to roam and ramble. I loved the smell of grapes, olives, and tomatoes clinging to trees and vines. I loved the warm laughter of the Italian people.

"My parents, though, were less overjoyed at my arrival. They were worried about me. 'What's the matter with you, Albert?' they asked again. 'You must start to get serious and plan for your future.' My future? I had no idea what that would be.

"Despite their disappointment, my parents were kind. They let me travel Italy and think before I had to decide my future. I visited Pisa and Siena, wandering past lovely old terra-cotta buildings and marveling at paintings and sculptures in museums. I walked through groves of gnarled olive trees and sun-drenched valleys and hills.

"And true to my promise, I became more serious after the trip"—Dr. Einstein took a sip of hot chocolate—"that is, I *tried* to be more serious."

"I took the entrance test for the famous Swiss Polytechnic Institute. But again I failed. I did well in math and science, but in nothing else. Now even I began to worry. Even *I* asked myself, What's the matter with you, Albert?

"But my family still believed in me, and they enrolled me in a wonderful school in Aarau, Switzerland. How I loved that school, Billy! It was relaxed and friendly. It was not all about drills and memorizing, but instead focused on ideas and thinking. I made many new friends there, and I took long hikes in the Swiss mountains. And that's when I decided to become a science teacher.

"I know that sounds strange to you now, even funny. Me, Albert Einstein, who always had such trouble in school? Me, Albert Einstein, the despair of teachers and principals? Me, Albert Einstein, the dreamy, disruptive boy whose bad attitude made teachers scream? Yes! Me! Albert Einstein wanted to become a teacher.

"I knew how important a good teacher is for students. And I knew how important it is for students to learn how to think and for teachers to encourage new ideas. I loved math and science, and I wanted to share that excitement with others. So I went back and took that polytechnic exam again.

"And this time, I passed. I was no longer a failure. I was starting to find my way!"

Dr. Einstein's face glowed. I knew that passing that exam meant a lot to him.

"My life was not all smooth and without bumps from then on," he continued, "but I did become a teacher and a scientist. I worked at what I love—math and science, especially the science of physics. I also learned to enjoy other things, such as sailing and playing the violin.

"Most of all, I continued to ask questions and look for answers. I developed theories and ideas. I even had a theory about the compass, that wonderful present my father gave me when I was five.

"Many people liked my theories. Some people even gave me important prizes and good jobs because of my ideas. The years passed, and now here I am, an old man—but an old man who is still working and learning. I even still love to play the violin.

"And sometimes people still say, 'What's the matter with Albert?' They say it when I'm absent-minded and lose my keys. They say it when I wear my funny old clothes and let my hair fly in all directions. But I know there's nothing the matter with me. It's just the way I am."

Dr. Einstein sat back in his chair, stretching his legs out in front of him.

"So tell me, Billy Whitestone, have I told you enough about me? Do you have any other questions?" Albert Einstein smiled again with those twinkly eyes of his.

Did I dare ask him anything else? I knew what Jane would say: "Go ahead, Billy. Ask! This may be your only chance."

So I did.

"I have four more questions, Dr. Einstein."

"Four?" said Albert Einstein, raising his eyebrows slightly. But the smile never left his face. "Well, well…. All right, Billy. Four questions."

These are my questions and Albert Einstein's answers:

Q1. Why don't you wear socks?

A1. When I was young I found out that the big toe always ends up making a hole in the sock. So I stopped wearing socks.

Q2. Why did your dog try to bite the mailman?

A2. The dog is very smart. He feels sorry for me because I receive so much mail. That's why he tries to bite the mailman.

Q3. What makes you think up all those great ideas?

A3. I use my imagination. Imagination is more important than knowledge. Knowledge is limited. Imagination encircles the world.

Q4. What's the most important thing to do in life?

A4. Never stop questioning. Never lose curiosity.

Right after my interview, I wrote down everything about Albert Einstein as a young man. I handed it to Jane the very next day.

"Surprisingly good," said Jane, almost smiling. "At least for the first part. Now write a follow-up article about what Albert Einstein accomplished when he grew up, and then you're done."

But I couldn't interview Dr. Einstein again. He was sick and couldn't have visitors. Instead, I researched the rest of the story in the library, using magazines, newspapers, and books. I called the second story "Albert Einstein: When He Grew Up."

This is what I wrote.

February 15, 1955

Albert Einstein
at age 70

Albert Einstein
When He Grew Up

By Billy Whitestone

In 1900, Albert Einstein graduated from the Swiss Polytechnic Institute. He wanted to teach, but he couldn't find a teaching job. For a year, he was so discouraged that he stopped thinking about science.

Finally, through friends, he found work in the patent office of Berne, Switzerland. His job was to study other people's inventions to see if they would work. Einstein liked analyzing a new invention, and soon he even started to think about his own science ideas again. The same questions he wondered about as a young boy still bothered him. How fast does light travel? What is the meaning of time? How old is the universe? He jotted down formulas. He explored ideas with his friends. He thought and he wondered and he finally came up with amazing new answers—so amazing that no one had proposed them before.

When he was twenty-six, he published several scientific papers. The third paper, called "The Special Theory of Relativity," was so original that it challenged the way people thought about science and the universe. Suddenly, Albert Einstein was not just a lowly patent clerk, but instead was a scientist everyone wanted to meet!

And soon the man who couldn't find a job teaching was offered many jobs. In 1909, he began teaching in Switzerland, and later he taught in Czechoslovakia and Germany.

In 1913, he developed another theory. This one, called the general theory of relativity, showed the relationship among mass, energy, and gravitation.

Photo of Albert Einstein riding his bike in Princeton, New Jersey

Eight years later, in 1921, Einstein was awarded the biggest physics prize of all, the Nobel Prize, for his work, especially the explanation of the law of photoelectric effect. Soon everyone was buzzing about Albert Einstein and his exciting ideas. His famous equation $E=mc^2$ became known around the world. Everyone wanted to meet the famous man who'd changed the way scientists viewed the universe.

Einstein and his second wife, Elsa, stayed in Germany until the early 1930s, when the Nazis came to power and passed laws against Jewish people. Einstein, who was Jewish, hated what the Nazis were doing. He also knew that staying in Germany was dangerous. So he moved with his family to Princeton, New Jersey. Einstein continued to work on physics in Princeton, but he also spent time working for world peace and freedom. He believed that before the world could find peace, it first had to defeat the terrible Nazis in Germany.

In 1945, the Nazis lost the war, and Einstein began talking about peace and freedom again. He believed that every human being should live in a free world where new ideas are encouraged and people feel safe to speak out.

Albert Einstein's most famous formula in his own handwriting

$$(E = mc^2)$$

I sent Albert Einstein a copy of the articles, with a card to thank him for talking to me and to say that I hoped he was feeling better. I was glad I did, for soon after, on April 18, 1955, Albert Einstein died. People said that beside his hospital bed lay math notes. He was working on problems even while he was sick. I wasn't surprised.

"Never stop questioning. Never lose curiosity," he had said.

And he never did.

Author's Note

Billy Whitestone is a made-up character, but Albert Einstein might have given someone like Billy an interview. Although he didn't like interviews, Einstein liked children. He liked their honest, open approach to what they saw, heard, and experienced.

The answers to Billy's four questions are in Einstein's own words. The rest of the story is based on factual biographical information, but the words are the author's, not Einstein's. Still, they have been written with Einstein's wise, funny personality and spirit in mind.

Important Dates in Albert Einstein's Life

1879   Albert Einstein is born to Hermann and Pauline Einstein, in Ulm, Germany, on March 14.

1880   His family moves to the big city of Munich, Germany.

1884   Einstein receives his first compass, which inspires his love of science.

1894   The Einsteins move from Munich to Italy, but Albert stays behind to finish school.

1896   Einstein graduates from high school and enrolls at the Swiss Polytechnic Institute in Zurich.

1902   Einstein begins a job at the Swiss patent office in Berne.

1903   Einstein marries Mileva Maric.

1905   Einstein publishes several important research papers, one on the special theory of relativity; he formulates the famous equation $E=mc^2$.

1906–16   Einstein's reputation in science grows, and he becomes a professor.

1914   The First World War begins.

1916   Einstein completes his general theory of relativity, which established the relationship among mass, energy, and gravitation.

1919	In May, a solar eclipse proves the general theory of relativity. Einstein and his first wife divorce, and he marries his cousin Elsa.
1922	Einstein wins the Nobel Prize for his work in physics, especially his explanation of the law of photoelectric effect.
1923	Einstein, by now world famous, visits many countries, encouraging people everywhere to live in peace. He promotes democracy and the free exchange of ideas, and begins to pursue his unified theory, an explanation for how the universe works.
1933	Dismayed by the rise of the Nazis in Germany, Einstein leaves Europe; he eventually settles in Princeton, New Jersey.
1936	His wife, Elsa, dies.
1939	The Second World War begins; Einstein warns the American president, Franklin Roosevelt, that the Nazis might be making weapons of mass destruction.
1945	The Second World War ends.
1946–55	Einstein campaigns against the destructive power of nuclear weapons and turns down an offer to become president of Israel; he continues to pursue his unified theory.
1955	Albert Einstein dies at seventy-six, in Princeton, on April 18.

**Anyone who has never made a mistake
has never tried anything new.**

—Albert Einstein